Please return/renew this item by the last date
shown. Books may be renewed by
telephoning, writing to or calling in at any
library or on the Internet.

Northamptonshire Libraries and Information Service

**Northamptonshire
County Council**

www.northamptonshire.gov.uk/leisure/libraries/

	BB	BV
BB	BD	BM
AG	BW	DX
JL		DM

Li Fu's Great Aim

The Inside Story of the Terracotta Archer

Karen Wallace

Illustrated by Helen Flook

A & C Black • London

To three warriors,
who know who they are

First published 2007 by
A & C Black Publishers Ltd
38 Soho Square, London, W1D 3HB

www.acblack.com

Text copyright © 2007 Karen Wallace
Illustrations copyright © 2007 Helen Flook

The rights of Karen Wallace and Helen Flook to be identified as
the author and illustrator of this work have been asserted by them
in accordance with the Copyrights, Designs and Patents Act 1988.

ISBN 978-1-4081-0402-6

A CIP catalogue for this book is available from the British Library.

This book is produced using paper that is made from wood
grown in managed, sustainable forests. It is natural, renewable and
recyclable. The logging and manufacturing processes conform
to the environmental regulations of the country of origin.

Printed and bound in Great Britain by MPG Books Limited.

Introduction

Xianyang, China, 219 BC

Confucius, the Chinese philosopher, once said: *A man who slays dragons must be a dragon himself.*

Of course, no one knew what he was talking about. Confucius said some pretty strange things. Years later, a thirteen-year-old boy called Zheng came to the throne of a land called Qin. He was a fierce fighter and wanted to conquer all the countries around him. What's more, Zheng didn't care how many noses he chopped off to do it.

He was a real dragon slayer.

Sure enough, Zheng got what he wanted. Twenty-five summers later, he ruled all the lands around him. Then, one day, he made an announcement. "I am Master of all under Heaven. From now on, all men will call me First Emperor."

It was the start of new times to come.

My name is Li Fu and I am a servant to the First Emperor. I know more of his secrets than any person alive. This is my story.

Chapter One

In the city of Xianyang, there is a huge marketplace with hundreds of stalls. Every morning, the Master of the Market beats a drum to tell the people business is open.

On the day my story begins, I was first through the gates. It was just after dawn, but I had to carry out an important errand. Well, two errands really. One for myself, and one for my master.

I wanted six new arrows and a bow so I could practise my archery.

It didn't take me long to find the right stall and buy what I needed.

"Anything else, Li Fu?" The man held up a flute and some bells. "Some music to soothe the emperor's temper, perhaps?" He gave me a sugar cake and winked.

I ate the cake and winked back. Everyone knows the emperor has a temper like a bull with a thorn up its nose. And he bellows like one, too.

"I need a tortoise shell," I replied.

"With tortoise inside for soup?" asked the man.

I shook my head.

"For reading omens, perhaps?"

I shrugged. My job is to keep the emperor's private life private. "For washing the Divine One's fingers."

The man smiled. We both knew I was lying. The emperor was obsessed by omens. It was common knowledge.

"Go down this alley," he said. "Turn right by the Temple of the Sky. There you will find many tortoise shells. Perfect for finger-washing."

✚ ✚ ✚

An hour later, I was on my knees in front of the First Emperor. To begin with, he said nothing. Then, after a mouthful of cooked wheat and honey, he made a low, growling noise.

I bowed my head nearer to the floor and pretended to stare at the yellow suns that were painted there. As Master of all under Heaven, the emperor liked to think of himself walking over all the suns in the universe. In fact, he liked to think he could walk over everyone and everything.

The emperor rattled the jade ornaments that hung from his belt. It was time to ask my first question of the day.

"Did the Divine One find peace in the land of sleep?" I murmured.

"Bad dreams," said the emperor in his hoarse, barking voice.

Of course, I couldn't look at him directly. No one was allowed to do that. But I could imagine the red-rimmed, almond-shaped eyes  that sloped upwards in his long face. He had a huge, hooked nose and his small, thick-lipped mouth was almost hidden by a moustache and beard.

"Bad dreams," said the emperor again, more loudly this time. He belched and threw his bowl of wheat across the floor.

I reached for the tiny harp I keep tucked in my coat, and played the tune I play every morning.

When I heard the huge man sit back, I put away my harp and waited.

Sure enough, the emperor hit a tiny gong with a hammer. It was the signal that he wanted the tortoise shell I had bought in the market. I took it from the canvas bag around my waist, and put it on the floor in front of him.

"You are a fine servant, Li Fu," said the emperor. "You understand my needs."

"It is my honour," I replied. And it *was* an honour to serve such a great master. It was also the only way I could earn his favour, and be awarded a place in his army like my brother.

"I must know the secrets of the tortoise shell," said the emperor.

As he spoke, I shuffled backwards on my knees. "Yes, Divine One. I will fetch the court wizard."

✦ ✦ ✦

The court wizard lived in a room on the top floor of the palace. Most nights, he stood on the roof and read the omens in the stars. Most mornings, if the omens were bad, he drank rice wine from a teapot.

When he opened his door, I could see that the omens were bad.

"The emperor commands your presence, court wizard," I said. "He wants the secrets of the tortoise shell."

The court wizard fixed me with his blackcurrant eyes. His face was thin and yellow behind his white whiskers. "Do you know why he calls for the tortoise shell to be read?"

"Bad dreams," I replied.

The wizard frowned. "How many nights?"

"Two."

The frown deepened. We both knew that dreams were seen as omens.

"Is the rod burning red in the fire?" asked the wizard.

I nodded. And we set off down the winding stairs.

Reading the tortoise shell was the job of the court wizard. He had to hold a hot iron to the shell just long enough for it to crack but not break. The cracks in the shell told the future.

The court wizard's knees were trembling as I walked behind him up to the emperor's chamber.

If I had been the court wizard, my knees would have trembled, too. They say bad omens come in threes.

Naturally, the emperor doesn't like to hear such things.

Chapter Two

My mother was making tea when I returned to our house.

I had been sent home because only the emperor and his advisors are allowed to hear the secrets of the tortoise shell. Even so, nothing stays secret at court for long, especially after the wizard has filled up his teapot. I would pay him a visit later that morning.

"Welcome, Li Fu," said my mother. Her dark eyes shone and she wore a red flower in her piled-up hair. It was a sign that something special had happened.

In the corner of the room was a suit of leather armour.

My heart sank. It could only mean one thing. My show-off older brother had come back from the war.

Sure enough, Chow swaggered into the room and settled himself down in front of the low table. It was as if he was master of the house.

"Still waiting like a silly maid on our emperor?" he sneered. He gulped the porcelain bowl of green tea and held it out for more. "You should be a soldier like me."

I ignored his insult. Besides, I knew that it was very unwise to speak in such words. Even walls have ears. Especially when they are made of paper, like ours.

"What thoughtless words, Chow," said my mother, quickly. She, too, knew the ways of the court. "Li Fu is a fine archer." She refilled Chow's bowl.  "The emperor keeps him by his side for the soothing music of his harp."

"Huh!" said Chow, leaning back on one arm. "Anyone can play a harp. You do not have to be brave and strong to pluck at tiny strings."

I felt my face go hot with anger. "One day I will be in the army!" I cried. "One day my arrows will pierce the hearts of the enemy on the battlefield!"

"The hearts of the sparrows in the courtyard, more like," said Chow. He held out his arm and clenched his fist. The muscles twisted like snakes under his skin. "Only yesterday, my sword cut through the neck of a Yan warrior."

"Where was this?" I asked, my anger turning to excitement. I couldn't help myself. My brother's stories of battles filled my mind with amazing pictures. I saw plains covered with thousands of soldiers rushing at each other, their weapons flashing in the sun. Galloping horses pulled chariots over the dusty ground. I saw generals beat out orders on their war drums. Orders to the archers. Orders to the crossbowmen. Orders to the soldiers.

Attack! *Attack*! *Attack*!

"One day, you will join your brother," said my mother, kindly. "One day, you will be the finest archer in the land." Her voice dropped. "Perhaps you will even be chosen for the army that will protect the emperor in the afterlife."

"Never!" shouted Chow, glaring at my mother. "Why should Li Fu have such an honour? It will be me!"

"Hush, Chow!" ordered my mother. "No one knows who will be chosen to march with the divine army. If it is the emperor's wish, you will join them."

Chow stared angrily at the floor. Everyone in the city was talking about the army that was to travel with the emperor to the afterlife. The warriors were made of red clay and were the size of real men. They carried proper, sharp weapons and every face was different.

Like a *real* army.

I stared at my brother. Would Chow be there with his thick, flat nose and low forehead, standing with his sword in his hands?

Already the craftsmen had made thousands of soldiers and archers and crossbowmen. There were wooden chariots, and horses made of bronze.

For a moment, no one spoke and I knew we were all thinking about the emperor's clay warriors.

It had been one of his first orders as Master of all under Heaven that such an army should be created. And not only warriors. All the court was to be there, from his senior officials and advisors to musicians and acrobats.

Naturally, I more than anyone knew how much the emperor worried about what would happen once he left this world for ever. He believed he still had to rule his kingdom. So, of course, he had to take his court and his army with him.

Then and there I sent up a prayer asking to be one of the emperor's warriors. If every face was different, what a honour it would be to have *my* likeness on the face of an archer. Then I could serve my master for ever!

My mother broke the silence. "We must all accept our fate," she said, and clapped her hands for our servant. "Come! You must both be hungry."

Chapter Three

The emperor believed that it was his duty to rule his kingdom with harsh punishments. If the people were terrified of him, then they would do as he commanded without protest. For that reason, his palace had been built to make men feel afraid.

His Great Chamber was at the top of very steep stairs, so that visitors became more and more nervous as they climbed upwards towards him.

The chamber itself was enormously high and filled with massive pillars, as many as there are trees in a forest.

Giant, whale-oil candles lit up the gold scales of the fierce dragons that were painted on the walls.

Behind the huge rooms, there were narrow passages for the servants to use without disturbing the court. As I made my way up one of these, I could hear the emperor bellowing, and the sound of his fist smashing down on a beaten metal table. His favourite word echoed around the Great Chamber.

NO! NO! NO!

I ran faster. I knew from the tone of his voice that the emperor was about to lose his temper and start to throw things. That was the moment his advisors always sent for me.

But first I had to find the court wizard. I had to know what he had seen in the cracks on the tortoise shell to understand what was *really* troubling my master.

I bounded up the rickety back steps like an antelope and pushed open the door to the court wizard's room.

It was empty.

My heart banged. *Now* what was I going to do? There was a tinkling sound. The doorway on to the roof was open, and the wind was rippling the strings of glass ornaments that hung from the ceiling.

I found the wizard lying flat on his face, his teapot clutched in his hand. Not far away was the tortoise shell with one end smashed. I didn't have to ask who had done that.

"Court wizard," I said, shaking the old man by his shoulders. "Wake up! You must help me."

The old man turned around, and I gasped. Half of his moustache had been chopped off and his beard had been cut from his chin. The poor man looked so ridiculous that I almost burst out laughing. Then I pinched myself hard.

The omens from the cracked tortoise shell must have been even worse than expected and the emperor had taken out his rage on the old wizard. It was cruel and unkind. Everyone knows that a man without his whiskers has no dignity.

"I know someone in the market," I said, gently. "He makes wigs from real hair. He'll fix you up." I put my hand on the wizard's arm. "The emperor forgets what he does in a temper."

"I understand. He fears the revenge of the gods in this life. He fears his own death." The wizard pointed to the broken shell. "And now there is more."

I ran over and picked up the shell. "What did you see? I am his close servant. Maybe I can protect him."

"You are a good boy, Li Fu," said the wizard. "But the secrets of the tortoise shell—"

I reached into my coat and found the flask I had brought from my mother's house. Then I tipped it into the wizard's teapot.

Sure enough, the secrets didn't stay secret for long.

✚ ✚ ✚

Half an hour later, I was sitting in my special hiding place behind the musicians' hall, forcing myself to think. What the court wizard had told me made no sense, and yet I knew there was a meaning if only I could see it.

The old man had held up the broken tortoise shell and pointed to the cracks caused by the touch of the hot iron. There was one long line with a sharp kink in it. At the point of the kink, there were lots of little cracks and breaks.

The wizard said they looked to him like musical notes, but he couldn't be sure, so he had said nothing to the emperor.

"See that line, boy." His bony finger had stabbed at the shell. "That is the emperor's life." Then he traced along the line to where it suddenly kinked. "This means that someone is going to try and kill him."

I felt cold shivers all over my body. "When?" I asked. "Can you tell?"

The old man had nodded and pointed to a mark that looked like a yellowish disc in the shell. "That's the full moon," he said in a hollow voice.

Now, as I sat with my head buried in the sleeves of my coat, I thought of that morning when I had risen before dawn. It had been dark and the moon was still guarding the sky. As the stars disappeared, I had looked up. The yellow disc was almost completely round.

Whoever was trying to kill the emperor would make his move tonight!

It was then I heard the sound of a musician tuning his harp. I knew it was a man called Zhang. He was one of the emperor's most favoured players. Indeed, that night Zhang and a young singer called Geji were to perform before him to celebrate the full moon.

Zhang was a brilliant player, and I let my thoughts slide as I listened to the tune he was playing. Then the strangest feeling came over me. The sound of the notes turned into the shapes of the tiny cracks on the tortoise shell.

As Zhang played, I took out my own little harp and plucked soundlessly on the strings. At the same time, I kept the picture of the cracks in my mind. The court wizard had been right! The little cracks *were* musical notes.

I put down my harp and heard my heart hammering in my chest. Could it be that Zhang's song was supposed to signal the emperor's death? If so, who could be the assassin? No one was allowed near the emperor with any kind of weapon. Not even a stitching needle.

Zhang only carried his harp, and Geji was always searched by a female servant before she stepped up the final flight of stairs.

I looked down at my little harp again. Instead of holding it with one hand and playing it with the fingers of the other, I held both ends of the curved frame and brought it down against my knee.

The blow was not strong.

Certainly, it would never crack a skull. Especially not the emperor's skull, which was said to be thicker than a buffalo's. So how could Zhang be the killer with only a harp for a weapon?

I shook my head and let out a deep breath. Before I could make a plan, I had to see Zhang's face. The look in his eyes would tell me what I needed to know.

Chapter Four

I took a short cut through the kitchens. The vast cauldrons hanging over crackling wood always amazed me. The ceiling was hung with hundreds of feathered game birds and two pigs were turning on a spit.

One of the cooks, Mi Wei, was a friend of our house cook and he always gave me a piece of fresh bread dipped in chilli pickles.

"Who is eating in the dining hall?" I asked, hearing the scraping of tables and the roar of voices.

"Tonight is full moon," said Mi Wei. "The musicians have been given a banquet by the emperor."

I swallowed my piece of bread and felt the chilli pickles turn fiery as they slipped down my throat. "May I make my greetings?"

Mi Wei shrugged. "You are a musician yourself."

I grinned and took his reply as a 'yes'. That's what I always do when no proper permission is given. I wiped my mouth and walked into the dining room.

One or two players called out and I smiled back, but the man I was looking for was at the far end of the room, surrounded by a small crowd of well-wishers.

"Li Fu!" cried Zhang when he saw me. His face was excited and there was a strange glitter in his eyes. He looked as if he had a fever. "I have been asking for you. I need your instruction."

I bowed. Such a request was a great honour.

"How can that be?" I asked politely. I looked away from his eyes so that he wouldn't think I was staring. "I am a poor musician."

"You play a *small* harp." Zhang took out a harp slightly bigger than mine from the folds of his coat. "Tonight, I shall play such an instrument before the emperor."

He plucked expertly at the strings and the room fell silent. A single high sound rang out, but it quickly faded away. "It is this note that I am finding difficult to play," said Zhang. "How do you do it?"

My blood froze. It was one of the notes on the tortoise shell.

"Please," said Zhang, handing me his harp. "Show me how with your fingers."

As I took the harp, I looked into his eyes. Now *they* were cunning. I had seen what I needed to know.

"It is easier like this," I explained in my most humble voice. "The little finger finds the note. The thumb holds it in place." As I handed him back his harp, I felt its weight. It was barely heavier than mine. It could never be a weapon.

Zhang bowed. "I am in your debt, Li Fu," he declared. He held out his hand. "I would be honoured if you joined our banquet."

However, I pleaded my duties to the emperor as an excuse to say no. And, as always, my excuse was accepted.

As I walked quickly back through the kitchen, I knew I had the answer to one of my questions.

It was Zhang *who* was going to try to kill the emperor that night.

But *how*?

I decided to return to the market. There was a harp maker I wanted to visit.

+ + +

The harp maker, Zhao Fu, was telling a story when I arrived at his stall. It was all about a stupid man who had paid a lot of money for a harp that was worthless.

"Who could have thought of such a thing?" Zhao Fu pulled a face and made a rude noise with his lips. "It was not a bronze frame. It was a tube."

"Maybe the man wanted it for a child," I suggested. "It would be light, at least."

"More like for a bird to play with its feet," replied Zhao Fu with another rude noise.

"So why did you make it?" I asked.

Zhao Fu shrugged. "He paid a big price." The harp maker sat down at his workbench and waved his listeners away. "Now I must work." He turned to me and smiled. As servant to the emperor, I was respected even though I was young. "Salutations to your house, Li Fu."

I bowed. "And yours, Zhao Fu."

A bell rang out for the early evening change of the royal guard. As I made my way quickly through the stalls, the smell of noodle broth wafted past me and I realised I was hungry.

My mother always says that a man's mind works best on a full stomach. There was just time to grab something to stuff in my mouth before I had to present myself at the Great Chamber.

As I walked to my favourite noodle stall, I passed a forge and watched as the blacksmith carefully poured a ladle of molten lead into a hollow clay pipe. When the lead cooled, and the clay was broken, there would be a short, heavy pole.

I thought of the harp with the hollow frame and suddenly everything made sense. A harp filled with lead would be heavy enough to smash anyone's skull.

Even the emperor's!

I forgot my hunger and began to run.

+ + +

"Gods' temples!" cried the court wizard, as he stepped into the hall. "There's no need to break down my door!"

I saw immediately that my friend in the market had done a brilliant job on the missing moustache and whiskers, and I was glad. I was going to need the court wizard's help.

"You must sit with the emperor while Zhang performs," said the court wizard when I had finished my story.

"But how can I do that?" I cried. "He has never invited me to join him before."

"Leave that to me," said the court wizard. "My job is to find omens. The emperor is so fearful at the moment, he will do as I tell him."

"But then what?" I asked. "How can I stop Zhang from attacking? He is strong, and I saw a wicked cunning in his eyes."

The court wizard opened a cupboard and handed me a small, silk pouch. "This is all you need."

Chapter Five

The emperor was dressed in fine robes of black and scarlet silk, with his curved sword fixed to his side. His thick hair was drawn up into a box-shaped headdress. A curtain of beads hung in front and behind his head so that his face was hidden.

I sat at his feet, desperately hoping that my own robes were thick enough to stop him from noticing that my knees were shaking like bulrushes in a breeze.

The emperor seemed calmer now that the court wizard had told him about the new omen, and had only grunted when I had taken my place.

"So, Li Fu," he whispered in his harsh voice. "You have found importance at last." He waggled his toes inside his embroidered slippers as if to underline his words. "A place by the emperor's feet is an honourable one."

I stared at the ground and whispered. "I give great thanks, your majesty"

Then something extraordinary happened. The emperor made a noise that sounded like a chuckle and said, "You please me, Li Fu."

Before I could think of any reply, he clapped his hands and I watched Zhang begin to climb up to the throne.

If I hadn't known what to look for, I would never have noticed that Zhang was carrying his harp in both hands. Normally, one hand is enough. But of course this harp was made of lead, and it was not for playing songs.

Then I realised that Zhang would not even begin to make music. How could he? The sound of the strings would give him away. His plan must be to attack the emperor as soon as he got close enough!

My hands were trembling as I felt for the silk pouch that was hidden in my sleeve. I worked it into my hand and loosened the tie with my fingers.

After that, everything happened very slowly. Zhang smiled and moved as lightly as a leopard towards the emperor. He bowed and I saw him change his grip on the harp.

The emperor nodded behind his curtain of beads. Then Zhang stood up. As he raised his arms, I jumped to my feet and threw the pouch full of pepper powder into his eyes.

There was a strangled cry. Zhang clutched at his face and the harp landed with a great *crash* on the marble floor and cracked a tile.

In that second, the emperor understood everything. He bellowed with rage and pulled the great sword from its case. Before his guards could reach him, he had brought it down on the back of Zhang's neck.

I have to say, it was not a pretty sight and at one moment, I thought I was going to be sick.

But in the end, I fainted instead.

✚ ✚ ✚

It was daylight when I opened my eyes. I was in my own house. The door opened and my mother walked in. To my astonishment, her eyes were brimming with tears, but she was smiling.

"Mother!" I sat up. "What has happened? Why are you crying?"

"You have been given a great honour, Li Fu," said my mother, wiping her cheeks. "Hurry, you must dress. The emperor commands your presence!"

✦ ✦ ✦

One of the royal guards met me at our front door and led me to a carriage. The shutters had been pulled down, so I had no idea where I was being taken. After what seemed like hours but was probably only 20 minutes, the carriage stopped and the door opened.

When I stepped down on to the dusty tiles, I couldn't believe my eyes. I was standing where few men had ever stood, beside the emperor's tomb. And for the first time, I saw the clay warriors.

There were thousands of them, so many that they seemed to stretch across the plains towards the mountains. There were soldiers on foot and soldiers on horses. There were crossbowmen and archers and, amongst them, horses with braided manes and tails pulled generals in chariots.

I stared until I thought my eyes would stick in their sockets. Then I stared some more. The colours of the uniforms gleamed in the early sun. There was green, red, lilac and purple. Even the armour was the glossy brown of polished leather.

Somewhere, a bell jingled. It was a signal that the emperor was approaching.

I fell to my knees.

A shadow passed over the ground and I knew that the emperor was standing above me.

"Li Fu," came his harsh voice. "You have done me a great service. I give thanks to the gods that they sent you to me last night."

I pressed my face to the ground and felt grit stick to my mouth. There was nothing I could say. I could only wait.

"Your mother tells me you are a fine archer," said the emperor. "That you want to fight like your brother." He grunted. "You will join my army on your next birthday."

I was so astonished that my head jerked upwards. Just in time, I brought it down again. "I am your emperor's devoted servant," I said, quickly, hoping he hadn't noticed my rudeness.

The emperor laughed. It was a strange bark of a laugh. "Li Fu, you may look up."

It was a moment I had often imagined, but had never ever believed *would* happen. To look into my master's face was a crime punishable by death. To my horror, I found I couldn't move my head. It was too scary.

Then I felt the emperor's hands on my chin. And the next thing I was looking into his great, black eyes.

"You are also to be an archer in my army of clay warriors," he said. "A young man who saves his emperor in one life may well do the same in the next."

And that was when I did something really strange. I threw myself at his feet and whooped with joy.

Well, it was all getting a bit much. Even for me.

✛ ✛ ✛

The emperor walked away, then I heard the wheels of his chariot rattle over the hard, dusty ground. Someone touched me and brought me to my feet. It was a man dressed in the costume of a court official. He led me across a small field to where groups of craftsmen were working on the faces of the clay warriors.

"Over there," said the man.

At first, I didn't understand. Then all the hairs lifted on the back of my neck. I was staring at an archer. He was kneeling, one leg on the ground, a bow in his hand. I could see his hair was drawn up and pulled to one side so the archer behind could see to take a shot. I looked at his face. It was me!

I opened my mouth to shout, but no sound came out. My prayer had been answered.

I would serve my emperor for ever!